This book belongs to:

_____

_____

Little Grey Rabbit's
Story Treasury

A TEMPLAR BOOK

This edition first published in the UK in 2013 by Templar Publishing,
an imprint of The Templar Company Limited,
Deepdene Lodge, Deepdene Avenue, Dorking, Surrey, RH5 4AT, UK
www.templarco.co.uk

The Squirrel, the Hare and the Little Grey Rabbit:
Original edition first published in the UK
in 1929 by William Heinemann
How Little Grey Rabbit Got Back Her Tail:
Original edition first published in the UK
in 1930 by William Heinemann
The Great Adventure of Hare:
Original edition first published in the UK
in 1931 by William Heinemann
The Story of Fuzzypeg the Hedgehog:
Original edition first published in the UK
in 1932 by William Heinemann
Squirrel Goes Skating:
Original edition first published in the UK
in 1934 by William Collins Sons & Co
Little Grey Rabbit's Christmas:
Original edition first published in the UK
in 1939 by William Collins Sons & Co

Text copyright © 2012 by the Alison Uttley Literary Property Trust
Illustration copyright © 2012 by the Estate of Margaret Tempest
Design copyright © 2013 by The Templar Company Limited

Photographs reproduced by kind permission of the
Alison Uttley Literary Property Trust and the Estate of Margaret Tempest

Cover illustration redesigned by Sophie Allsopp

This edition edited by *Susan Dickinson* and *Hannah Pang*
Designed by *janie louise hunt*

1 3 5 7 9 10 8 6 4 2

ISBN 978-1-84877-869-6

Printed in China

Little Grey Rabbit's Story Treasury

By Alison Uttley
Pictures by Margaret Tempest

templar publishing

Contents

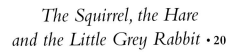

A Note from the Editor

Editor Susan Dickinson worked on numerous
editions of the original Little Grey Rabbit books.
Here she talks about her experiences of being
involved with the stories that have captured
the hearts of generations…

*Working with Alison Uttley and Margaret Tempest was
a privilege and a pleasure. I had been familiar with the Little
Grey Rabbit books since childhood — my sister and I used
to copy some of the illustrations from* Little Grey Rabbit's
Christmas *when we were making our own Christmas cards.*

I joined William Collins in 1960 as Editor of Children's Books and inherited an outstanding list of authors and artists – among them Alison and Margaret, both of whom were now quite elderly, but still very creative. I went out to Beaconsfield, Buckinghamshire, to meet Alison in her home. The house was unmistakably 'Alison'. There was a special feel to it: lovely old furniture, Dutch paintings, a largish garden with a row of dogs' graves at the bottom. Margaret lived in Ipswich, Suffolk. She and her brother Frank had been friends with Arthur Ransome (author of the Swallows and Amazons series) and they had all gone sailing together on the Broads. Alison's background was rooted in the country and in country ways.

Both Alison and Margaret were fiercely passionate about
the books. Each believed she had created the characters.
Alison of course had first written the stories of Squirrel, Hare
and Little Grey Rabbit, the Hedgehog family, Wise Owl,
Postman Robin and Moldy Warp the Mole. (The animals
were in all probability based on people Alison knew.)
Margaret had created their visual images. When we think
of them, we see them as she drew them. But we also see
their characters as Alison intended them.

The first four books were published by Heinemann and
it was someone in the Heinemann office who brought these
two talented ladies together. Then in 1934 William Collins
took over as the publisher of Little Grey Rabbit. New titles
were added regularly. When I arrived in the Collins' offices

*a new Little Grey Rabbit story was expected annually. Being
Alison Uttley's editor was always interesting. She was
someone who had to be treated with great care and tact, and
I often found myself visiting her home in Beaconsfield with
a new batch of illustrations. Sometimes, something needed to
be changed and this had to be handled very carefully with
Margaret who also loved each character dearly. But it was
fun. The size of the books has been consistent throughout
their life, although the cover design has changed occasionally.
I feel proud to have been involved.*

Susan Dickinson.

Susan Dickinson, 2013

About
the Author

*"Why do children love them? Because I believe
in them. Mine aren't made up. They are real…
I don't sit down to write a story, they come."
– Alison Uttley, writing about her characters.*

*Alison Uttley's Little Grey Rabbit series has been loved by millions
and continues to be popular to this day. The first book in the series
was published in 1929; entitled* The Squirrel, the Hare and the
Little Grey Rabbit.

*A talented writer and a best-selling author of children's books,
Alison Uttley (born Alice Jane Taylor in 1884) grew up on Castle
Top Farm, overlooking the Derwent Valley in Derbyshire. It was here
that she gathered so much of the inspiration for her countryside tales.*

*Alison was educated at the Lea School in Holloway and the Lady
Manners School in Bakewell, where she developed a love for science.
This led to a scholarship at Manchester University, where in 1906 she
became the second woman to graduate with an honours degree in physics.
She went on to study education at Cambridge before becoming
a teacher. In 1911, she married a scientist called James Uttley,
who tragically died in 1930. The couple had one son, and*

in a bid for financial security, Alison turned her writing talents into a livelihood that would enable her to support him. She did so by creating numerous series of animal tales including the Little Grey Rabbit, the Little Red Fox, Sam Pig and Tim Rabbit.

She also wrote a number of books for older children and adults, including The Country Child (1931), a reflection on her own country childhood. It was the first of many books about the countryside, which would lead Alison on to become an admired writer of rural essays, in which she was able to recall the smallest details from her Derbyshire childhood with poetic skill. She published a cookery book, Recipes from an Old Farmhouse, as well as a fantasy, A Traveller in Time, centred on the Babington Plot to put Mary Queen of Scots on the English throne.

Alison was a talented writer and in the Little Grey Rabbit series she brings together many of the ingredients that continue to make it a success including vivid descriptions of an animal community who always strive to overcome their problems with a sense of goodwill.

Eventually settling in Beaconsfield, Alison Uttley wrote over one hundred books in her lifetime and, in 1970, was given an honorary Doctor of Letters degree by Manchester University as a recognition of her literary achievements. She died on 7th May 1976, aged 91.

About the Artist

Margaret Tempest's working relationship with Alison Uttley lasted for forty years, and her unique eye for interpretation brought the warm and touching world of Little Grey Rabbit and her friends vividly to life.

Margaret was born in 1892, into a well-known Ipswich family: her father served as mayor of Ipswich when she was little, her elder brother Roger was rector of nearby Kersey, and her younger brother Frank, a solicitor, also followed in their father's footsteps to become mayor.

From an early age, she showed a talent for drawing and attended the art school in Ipswich before going on to the Westminster School of Art in 1914. From there she co-founded and was secretary of the Chelsea Illustrators Club, a group of former students who set up a studio off the King's Road in London. They made their business a success by putting on yearly exhibitions between 1919 and 1939, where they sold their work, as well as producing commercial material such as Christmas cards. Margaret also did freelance teaching around the Hertfordshire area, where the British ornithologist and founder of the World Wildlife Fund, Peter Scott, was one of her pupils.

Margaret began illustrating Alison Uttley's Little Grey Rabbit books in 1929 and continued to do so into the 1960s. She also wrote and illustrated a number of other children's books including the Curly Cobbler and Pinkie Mouse series as well as some religious titles: she also designed picture postcards for the Medici Galleries in London.

Her marriage late in life to Sir Grimwood Mears, a former Chief Justice in Allahabad, India, lasted until his death in 1963. Sadly, the onset of Parkinson's disease prevented Margaret from being able to draw in her latter years, and she died in 1982, aged 90.

Margaret Tempest was a fine artist, and her illustrations played a vital part in the appeal of the Little Grey Rabbit books. She was known to have a delightful way with children: sitting each one on her lap, she would ask which animal they liked best, and proceed to draw it for them.

We would like to think that Alison Uttley and Margaret Tempest would have taken great pleasure from the knowledge that a new generation of readers will now be transported back into the nostalgic country ways of Little Grey Rabbit's world…

Foreword

Of course you must understand that Grey Rabbit's home
had no electric light or gas, and even the candles were made
from pith of rushes dipped in wax from the wild bees' nests,
which Squirrel found. Water there was in plenty, but it did
not come from a tap. It flowed from a spring outside, which
rose up from the ground and went to a brook. Grey Rabbit
cooked on a fire, but it was a wood fire, there was no coal in
that part of the country. Tea did not come from India, but
from a little herb known very well to country people, who
once dried it and used it in their cottage homes. Bread was

baked from wheat ears, ground fine, and Hare and Grey Rabbit gleaned in the cornfields to get the wheat.

The doormats were plaited rushes, like country-made mats, and cushions were stuffed with wool gathered from the hedges where sheep pushed through the thorns. As for the looking-glass, Grey Rabbit found the glass, dropped from a lady's handbag, and Mole made a frame for it. Usually the animals gazed at themselves in the still pools as so many country children have done. The country ways of Grey Rabbit were the country ways known to the author.

A.U.

Meet the Main Characters

Little Grey Rabbit

Little Grey Rabbit is a lovable caring mother figure who looks after her two friends Squirrel and Hare by shopping, cooking and baking. She always wears a grey dress with white collar and cuffs, which she protects with her blue apron when doing the housework. She wraps up in a blue cloak or a red muffler in cold weather, and saves her cobweb scarf and silver birch slippers for special occasions.

Hare

Hare lives in the little house on the edge of the wood with Little Grey Rabbit and Squirrel. A boastful yet lovable fellow, Hare rarely thinks things through. Such impulsiveness means he often finds himself at the centre of one calamity or another. Hare likes to dress smartly, wearing a blue coat on weekdays and a red coat on Sundays and special occasions.

Squirrel

Squirrel is a proud and vain character with a kind heart. She enjoys looking at her own reflection and wearing pretty ribbons. She usually wears a pale brown dress with darker spots, complete with yellow neck frill and yellow frilled cuffs. She wears a green dress in winter and on special occasions dons her tail with a green bow to match.

HEDGEHOG
Milkman Hedgehog is an honest,
hard-working fellow. He milks the cows
and delivers it to the community of animals.

MRS HEDGEHOG
Hedgehog's wife is a good mother to their little son Fuzzypeg, and
makes sure that Hedgehog is always presentable for work.

FUZZYPEG
An adventurous child, Fuzzypeg adores Little Grey Rabbit and
pays her many a visit. He enjoys going to school and is keen to learn.

POSTMAN ROBIN
Robin is the local postman who not only delivers the
letters, but also carries the latest news and observations
on the wing.

MOLDY WARP
Moldy Warp is a kind, caring mole who likes to make
and collect interesting things. His cosy, underground
house is not too far from Little Grey Rabbit's home.

WISE OWL
As his name suggests, Wise Owl is a source
of information for the local animals. He can be
aggressive when disturbed but will often solve
a problem, and usually wants something in return.

*Little Grey Rabbit lives with her friends
Squirrel and Hare in a little house at the edge of the wood.
One day, a fearsome weasel arrives, threatening the safe,
cosy lives of the woodland animals. Little Grey Rabbit
must use all of her courage and cunning if she is
to outwit the weasel and save her friends.*

THE SQUIRREL,
THE HARE AND THE
LITTLE GREY RABBIT

ALONG TIME AGO, in a little house on the edge of a wood, there lived a hare, a squirrel and a little grey rabbit.

The hare, who wore a blue coat on weekdays and a red coat on Sundays, was a conceited fellow.

The squirrel, who wore a brown dress on weekdays and a yellow dress on Sundays, was proud.

But the little rabbit, who always wore a dress with a white collar and cuffs, was not proud at all.

Every morning, when the birds began to twitter, she sprang out of her bed in the attic and ran downstairs to the kitchen. She went into the shed for firewood, and lit the fire. Then she filled her kettle with clear water from the brook that ran past the door, just beyond the garden.

While the water boiled she swept the floor and dusted the kitchen. She made tea from daisy-heads in a brown teapot. Then she laid the table, put a bunch of lettuce leaves on each plate, and called Squirrel and Hare.

"Squirrel, Hare, wake up – breakfast is ready!"

Downstairs they strolled, rubbing their eyes and wriggling their ears.

"Good morning, Grey Rabbit," yawned Hare. "I declare you have given us lettuce again. Really, my dear, you must think of something new for breakfast."

"Good morning, Grey Rabbit," said Squirrel. "Where's the milk?"

"It hasn't come yet," she said.

"Tut," exclaimed Squirrel. "Late again."

Just then there was a tapping at the door. Little Grey Rabbit ran to open it, and there stood Hedgehog with a pint of milk.

"I nearly didn't get here at all," he said. "A dreadful thing has happened! A weasel has come to live in the wood. It isn't safe to be out after dusk."

"Oh dear!" replied Grey Rabbit. "You must take care you don't get caught, even if we *do* go without milk."

"Bless your heart," smiled Hedgehog. "You shall have milk as long as old Hedgehog has some prickles left. Well, good day, and warn those two grumblers in there."

"Whatever have you been talking about all this time?" asked Squirrel angrily.

Little Grey Rabbit drew her chair close. "Hedgehog says a weasel has come to live in the wood."

"A weasel?" said Squirrel. "Pooh! Who's afraid of a weasel?"

But she shut the window and poked the fire, and kept the poker in her hand while she drank her milk.

A *tap, tap, tap* came on the door.

"Who's that?" asked Squirrel.

Grey Rabbit opened the door a crack. "It's only Robin Redbreast with the letters," cried she. "Come in Robin, you quite startled us. Have you heard the news?"

"About the weasel? Yes. He's a great big fellow with very sharp teeth. Well, I must be off, I have to warn the birds," he said, and away he flew.

"Oh dear," said Grey Rabbit. "Perhaps I'd better not go out today."

"But I need a new teasel brush," cried Squirrel. "My tail is quite tangled."

"And I want some carrots," said Hare. "I'm tired of lettuce for breakfast."

So Little Grey Rabbit set off, with her basket on her arm. She kept a sharp lookout in the wood, and ran so softly that the leaves underfoot scarcely moved.

She found some teasel bushes growing in the hedge. She bit off three prickly heads and put them in her basket.

Then she ran on till she got to the farmer's garden. One by one, she carefully pulled up some carrots and placed them in her basket.

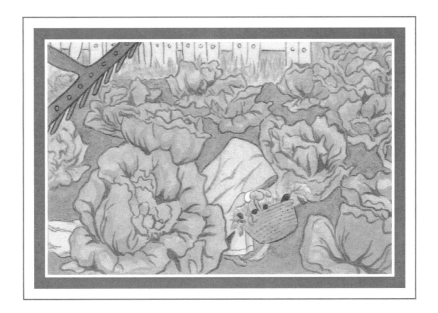

"I wish we could grow carrots at home," she said.

Suddenly, she heard an angry shout. A sack was thrown over her head and someone hit wildly at her with a rake.

Little Grey Rabbit ran this way and that as she tried to dodge the blows. Then she darted out through a hole in the sack. She ducked in and out of the cabbage leaves, with the farmer running after, close to her heels.

"You little rascal!" called the farmer. "You've been after my carrots. Just wait till I catch you."

But Little Grey Rabbit did not wait. She could not stop to explain that she thought they were everybody's carrots. She ran for her life, across the field to the wood.

"I don't think I shall go there again," she said, as she put a dock-leaf bandage on her hurt paw. "We must grow our own carrots. I will ask Wise Owl how to do it."

She hurried through the wood, and reached home safely.

"What a long time you have been," grumbled Hare. "Did you get my carrots?"

Little Grey Rabbit cooked dinner and gathered firewood. She was never still for a moment, but Hare and Squirrel sat beside the fire and never moved except to put fresh wood on the blaze.

When Hare and Squirrel had gone to bed, Little Grey Rabbit slipped outside. The moon was big and the stars winked and smiled at her. Everywhere was silver white, and Little Grey Rabbit could not help turning head over heels for joy.

She jumped the brook three times, then trotted into the wood. She noticed her feet left a trail of footprints in the grass, so she turned round and walked backwards.

At last she reached Wise Owl's house, a hollow oak tree. He sat on a bough, his shining eyes searching the wood.

Little Grey Rabbit waved a white handkerchief for a truce, and he nodded down at her.

"Wise Owl," she began, "will you tell me how to grow carrots?"

"What will you give me in return?" hooted Wise Owl.

"Oh dear, I haven't anything," she said sadly.

"Yes, you have," cried Owl. "You can give me your tail."

"My tail?" she exclaimed in horror.

"Yes, your tail," said Wise Owl, "or I shall not help you."

"You can have it," Little Grey Rabbit cried bravely. "But be quick."

So Wise Owl hopped down and, with one bite of his strong beak, he cut it off. Then he fastened it on his front door as a door knocker.

"You can grow carrots with carrot seed," he said.

"Where can I get it?" asked Little Grey Rabbit.

"From the shop in the village." Then he flapped his wings and flew away.

Little Grey Rabbit started for home. Now and then a shiny round tear fell on the grass, and she gave a sigh.

Suddenly, she turned a corner and saw the weasel! His back was turned; he was examining her footprints.

"Ah!" he cried. "A rabbit has gone this way!"

The weasel followed the footprints towards the brook, but when he reached it he was puzzled, for the footprints ran towards the water's edge on both sides. He scratched his whiskers.

"She must have tumbled in and been drowned," he said, and went off down the stream.

Little Grey Rabbit ran home and slept till the birds began to sing.

In the morning Hare stared at her. "Whatever have you done with your tail?" he asked.

"I gave it to Wise Owl," said Grey Rabbit, hanging her head.

"Disgraceful," said Hare.

"Disgracefuller," said Squirrel, not to be outdone.

A big tear ran down into Grey Rabbit's tea. She wished Wise Owl would give her back her tail.

After dinner she set off for the village, leaving Squirrel and Hare dozing by the fire. They did not see her go, nor did they see a black nose appear at the window.

When Little Grey Rabbit got to the village it was very quiet. No one saw her hesitate a moment outside the shop, then run through the open door.

She gazed about her with wide-open eyes. Wonderful things lay all about: buckets and frying pans, pots and cheeses, mouse-traps and cherry brandy. But would she ever find the seeds? Then she saw a picture of a carrot on a little packet, lying with other packets. Success at last! Here were lettuces and radishes, parsley and cabbages.

She seized one of each. Then she saw a bag with a yellow bird on it labelled 'Canary Seed', so she took that too.

As she ran home, she made her plans. "I shall sow three rows of carrot seeds, and the radishes next to them, and the parsley next. Then I'll sow the bird seed and have some little yellow birds as well."

She ran down the street and saw no one, except for five ducks waddling across the road.

"Ah," she went on, "I may get hundreds and hundreds of little birds from this bag... Goodness me, what's this?" For she had reached home and the front door stood wide open. No one was there.

In the kitchen the chairs were upset and the table pushed on one side. Bits of red hair from Squirrel's tail lay on the floor.

"Oh my dear Squirrel, my darling Hare," she cried, tears running down her cheeks. "Has that bad weasel got you?"

She took a pair of scissors, a rope and a stick, and started out to look for her companions.

On the other side of the brook the grass was flattened, as if a heavy object had been pulled along.

"He has put them in a bag and dragged them home," she murmured. "Poor, poor things!"

She hurried along the path, which took her through dark and gloomy glades. At last she came to an ugly black house with thick smoke coming out of the chimney.

She lay down under a bush and waited.

Soon the door opened and the savage weasel stood in the doorway.

"I shall need more sticks for the fire after all," he said. "They will be safe in there."

He shut the door and turned the key in the lock, then ran among the bushes, picking up sticks.

"Too-whit, too-whoo," called Wise Owl, as he flew overhead. The weasel looked up. He was afraid of Wise Owl, and he dared not move.

Grey Rabbit made a dash, turned the key, and was in the house while the weasel still gazed up at the owl overhead.

Little Grey Rabbit called, "Hare, Squirrel, where are you? It's me, it's Rabbit."

"Here, here! Oh save us, dear Grey Rabbit," cried two piteous voices from a bag under the sofa.

Quickly Rabbit cut the bag open and let the two unhappy ones out, but they were so bruised and weak they could hardly walk.

"Upstairs with you," cried Grey Rabbit, as she heard the weasel returning. "Take this rope and let yourselves out of the window. I will follow."

Then she seized a stool and crept into the bag, just as the weasel came in.

Grey Rabbit squeaked and moaned, and the weasel chuckled as he piled wood on the fire.

Upstairs Squirrel and Hare fastened the rope to a bedpost and slid down into the nettles. Away they went, struggling over brambles and across ditches.

The weasel opened the oven door, putting some dripping in the roasting tin. "I'll cook them both together," he said.

He took a stick and came over to the bag. Then he raised the stick and – *bang!* – down it came. Grey Rabbit crept inside the stool and lay protected by its legs. She didn't make a sound.

"Dead, both dead," said the weasel.

As he took hold of the hot roasting tin, Grey Rabbit slipped out of the bag, gave him a great push into the tin, and shut the oven door.

Off she ran, never stopping till she got home. As she sat panting in an armchair, the other two limped in.

"Oh, Grey Rabbit," they said, "we are very sorry. We shall never be proud or rude again. You saved us from the weasel, and if he ever comes back—"

"He won't, he is roasted by now," she interrupted, and told them all her adventures.

So they all lived happily together, and had a fine crop of radishes, carrots and onions, but no little yellow birds ever came up.

And sometime, I will tell you how
Grey Rabbit got her tail back again…

The End

LITTLE GREY RABBIT'S tail is missing – she gave it
to Wise Owl to use for a door knocker, and he won't give
it back. In this story, her friends decide to help her retrieve it.
Join Little Grey Rabbit, Squirrel, Hare and kind old
Moldy Warp the Mole in this heart-warming tale
about the resourcefulness of loyal friends.

HOW
LITTLE GREY RABBIT
GOT BACK HER TAIL

ONE COLD MARCH MORNING, Little Grey Rabbit awoke at dawn, for this was to be a busy day.

Softly she opened her door and listened. Snores could be heard coming from Hare's room, and squeaky little grunts from Squirrel's.

She crept downstairs, took down a round wicker basket and went out into the raw air.

The sun had not yet risen, and a single star still shone in the sky, "like a candle for a little rabbit," she thought.

As she walked down the garden path she looked back at the shut windows and waved a paw to her sleeping friends in the little house.

She turned down the lane and scampered over the stones, leaping over thorny briars and swinging her basket round and round above her head.

A startled mouse gazed after her.
"I wonder where she is going? It's a pity she's lost her tail.
They say it is fastened on Wise Owl's door as a knocker."

Grey Rabbit came to an opening in a hedge and climbed through, tearing her apron on a thorn. She stopped to pin it with a pin from a hawthorn bush, and to sip some water from a gurgling spring, like a small fountain in the grass.

Then she ran across the meadow to a bank where the first primroses were growing. She began to pick them, biting off their pink stalks, and filling her basket with yellow blossoms.

Suddenly a black nose and two pink hands poked up in front of her.

"Oh! Oh! Moldy Warp, how you frightened me!" she exclaimed, with her paw on her fluttering heart.

"What are you doing out here so early, Grey Rabbit?" asked the mole.

"I am picking primroses for primrose wine. Hare has a bad cold and it is a certain cure."

"What a clever rabbit you are!" said Moldy Warp admiringly. "But where is your tail?"

"I gave it to Wise Owl," she replied. "He told me where to get carrot seed."

"Oh! He did, did he?" muttered the mole. "Grey Rabbit, would you like your tail back very much?"

"Very, very much," answered Grey Rabbit sadly.

"I'll help you," said the mole, just as a long sunray shone across the field and turned his velvet waistcoat red. "I will think out a plan."

"Thank you, Moldy Warp. I must run now, or I shall be late for breakfast." And off she went with her flowers bobbing up and down in the basket.

In the little house by the wood, Squirrel and Hare couldn't find Little Grey Rabbit anywhere.

Hare ran up and down stairs with his head in a red cotton handkerchief, calling, "Where are you, Grey Rabbit? A-tishoo! Are you hiding? A-tishoo!"

But Squirrel saw Grey Rabbit's basket was gone, and guessed she must be busy somewhere.

"Help me to get the breakfast, Hare," she scolded.

Hare wiped his eyes and sneezed violently. "A-tishoo!" he went, then he swept the tablecloth off the table and wrapped it round his shoulders.

"Oh, do be careful!" exclaimed Squirrel, seizing the cloth and shaking it.

Just then, there was a *rat-a-tat-tat* at the door. It was Hedgehog with the milk.

"Late again!" said Squirrel. "Have you seen Grey Rabbit?"

Hedgehog shook his old head. "No," said he. "Is she missing?"

"Of course she is, or I should not ask you," snapped Squirrel.

"Sorry, no offence," said Hedgehog, picking up his milk cans. "I can't abide that pair," he muttered as he set off. "Now, Grey Rabbit is a nice little thing."

He heard light footsteps coming up the lane, and a voice singing:

> "Primroses, primroses,
> Primroses fine,
> Pick them and press them
> And make yellow wine."

"Good morning, Hedgehog!" said Grey Rabbit, as she ran to the house. "Hare! Squirrel! Look at my primroses, picked with dew on them. Now we can make primrose wine to cure your cold, Hare!"

All day long they made the wine. Grey Rabbit packed the primroses in a wooden cask. Between each layer she put an acorn-cup of honey and a squeeze of wood-sorrel juice.

Squirrel filled the kettle from the brook and put it on the fire. Grey Rabbit poured boiling water over the flowers until the cask was full. Then she sealed it with beeswax and buried it in the garden.

"When can we have some?" asked Hare, as they sat down to tea.

"In twenty-four hours," said Little Grey Rabbit, and Hare began counting the minutes.

That night, Wise Owl flew over the house.

"Too-whit, a-tishoo!" he cried. "Too-whoo, a-tishoo!"

"Poor Wise Owl," murmured Grey Rabbit, tucked in her blanket. "He has a cold too. I must take him a bottle of primrose wine."

The next day, Squirrel worked in the garden, sowing fresh dandelion and lettuce seeds.

Hare sat sneezing by the fire, playing noughts and crosses against himself. He always won, so he was happy.

Little Grey Rabbit sat in her rocking chair mending her torn apron.

At last Squirrel came in, stamping her feet.

"It's bitter today, Grey Rabbit. And look at my tail! Where's my teasel brush? It's time you got me another."

After dinner, Grey Rabbit left Hare explaining noughts and crosses to Squirrel, who could never understand.

Away she went, through the wood with her basket. She stopped to look longingly at a horse-chestnut tree whose sticky buds were beyond her reach.

Then she ran through the gate and into the teasel field, where she bit off some prickly teasel heads and put them in her basket.

Home she ran, stepping on the soft moss.

"Robin Redbreast has been with a letter for you," said Squirrel.

Grey Rabbit took the leaf-envelope and broke open the brown flap.

"It's Moldy Warp's writing," she said. "It reads 'Found Knock Mole'."

"Whatever can it mean?" they all asked.

Hare said, "Moldy Warp has been found knocked over."

Squirrel said, "Mr Knock has found a mole."

Grey Rabbit said, "Mole has found a knock, but who has lost one?"

As evening wore on, Hare got more and more excited, until he could hardly bear to wait to dig up the cask of primrose wine.

When the seals were at last broken, such a delicious smell came into the room, like pine forests and honeysuckle and lime trees in flower. They filled their glasses with the golden wine.

"Good, good," said Hare. "I feel better already."

Then Little Grey Rabbit filled a bottle and tucked it under her arm to take to Wise Owl.

It was dark and the wood was full of rustles and murmurs. Grey Rabbit felt very frightened, for they were not comfortable, homely sounds.

"A-tishoo! A-tishoo!" came echoing through the trees, and Grey Rabbit caught sight of Owl. And her own little white tail was hanging on his front door.

"I've brought you some primrose wine for your sneeze," she said.

"Thank you kindly, Grey Rabbit. What would you like in return?"

Little Grey Rabbit hesitated and looked at her tail.

"No, I could not part with that. Not unless you bring me a bell to go *ting-a-ling-ling* when visitors call. But here is a book of riddles for you."

Grey Rabbit ran home with the book in her paw, but her thoughts full of the bell.

Squirrel and Hare were waiting for her, and between them, sipping from a teacup, sat Moldy Warp.

"Here she comes! Mole has something for you," exclaimed Hare.

Mole brought out a large silver penny. "It's Roman," he said. "I thought it would do for Wise Owl's door knocker."

"Oh, Moldy Warp, how kind. But Wise Owl will only give me back my tail in exchange for a bell."

"A bell? Where can we get a bell?" wondered Moldy Warp.

"There's a bell in the village shop," remembered Grey Rabbit.

"There are harebells, bluebells and Canterbury bells in the fields," said Hare.

"I might make a bell," said the mole, holding the penny in his strong hands. "I will bend it and twist it with my fingers till—"

And he walked musingly out of the house.

"Good night!" everyone called after him, but he only said, "And bend it and twist it," as he went slowly down the garden path.

Hare took the book of riddles to bed with him, and prepared to astonish Squirrel with a joke.

But when he awoke without his *a-tishoo*, he felt so grateful to Grey Rabbit that he got up early and went out into the fields to look for bells.

After breakfast, Squirrel announced, "I'm going to the village shop to get that bell."

"Oh, Squirrel!" exclaimed Grey Rabbit. "Please don't. The old woman might catch you."

But Squirrel put on her best yellow dress and her little blue shoes, and tied her tail with a bow of blue ribbon. Then she ran with a hop and a skip down the lane until she reached the village.

Presently a woman came out of a cottage and pushed open the shop door. *Tinkle, tinkle* went the bell, as Squirrel darted inside.

She leaped up and landed on the bell, which jangled loudly as it swung to and fro. She kicked her shoes off and lost her blue bow as she bit and tugged and pushed. At last the bell, with Squirrel still hanging onto it, fell to the floor, knocking over three buckets and a basket of eggs.

The shopkeeper shrieked. "That creature has got my bell!" she cried.

Squirrel picked up the noisy bell and ran out of the door, jingle-jangling through the market-place. She banged and bumped along the road, up the lane, through the garden and into the house.

Squirrel was a heroine that day.

But when Hare and Grey Rabbit dragged the bell across the wood to Wise Owl's door, he put his head out with half-shut eyes and hooted, "Who's making all that hullabaloo? How can I sleep with that jingle-jangle? Take it away!" And he slammed his door so that the little white tail shook.

When the dejected Hare and Grey Rabbit got home they found Moldy Warp talking to Squirrel.

He had brought a little silver bell made from the old coin. It had a tiny clapper of a hawthorn stone hung on a hair from a white mare's tail. When Moldy Warp shook the bell, a sweet silvery tinkle came from it.

Grey Rabbit started off to see Wise Owl as soon as it was dusk. She felt no fear as she carried the bell through the wood, for the wood held its breath to listen.

"What is that?" asked Wise Owl, as he peered down from his branch.

"A bell for my tail," said Grey Rabbit boldly, and she tinkled the little silver bell.

Owl climbed down. "You shall have your tail, Grey Rabbit. Give me the bell. It is beautiful, and it is wise, for it lived in the beginning of the world."

He hung the bell on his front door, and gave Grey Rabbit her tail in exchange, fastening it on with threads of stitchwort. By the time Little Grey Rabbit reached home again her tail was as good as ever.

Moldy Warp smiled, and took with him to his house under the green fields a bottle of primrose wine and the thanks of them all.

The End

ONE DAY, brave Hare leaves his friends
Little Grey Rabbit and Squirrel in their cosy house
at the edge of the wood and sets off to visit Toad on the
other side of the valley. On the way, he meets a charming
gentleman with a red coat and a bushy red tail...
Will Hare survive to tell the tale of his great adventure?

THE
GREAT ADVENTURE
OF HARE

IT WAS A LOVELY midsummer morning, and Hare looked out of his bedroom window onto the fields where cloud shadows were running races.

Green-blue butterflies and fierce little wasps flew among the flowers in the garden below. Hare stroked his whiskers and said, "Just the day for my adventure."

"Grey Rabbit, Grey Rabbit, come here," he called over the banisters, "and bring my walking stick, will you?"

Grey Rabbit ran upstairs with a cherry-wood stick and
a teasel brush.

Hare took down his new blue coat from the hook behind
the bedroom door. He put it on, with Grey Rabbit's help,
twisting his head to get a good view of the two brass buttons
at the back.

Grey Rabbit brushed off some tiny specks of whitewash
with her teasel brush. She had to stand on tiptoes to reach
Hare's shoulders, she was so small.

"Are my buttons all right?" asked Hare.

"Yes, like two looking glasses," replied Grey Rabbit, as she gave each one a rub with a duster, and then peeped at her face in the dazzling buttons.

"Don't forget your watch," she added, as Hare started downstairs.

"Oh dear, how careless you are, Grey Rabbit," said Hare, taking a large silver watch from the chest of drawers and putting it in his waistcoat pocket. "I nearly went without it."

"Goodbye, Squirrel," called Hare, as Squirrel looked up from the mittens she was knitting. "I'm off on my great journey. Goodbye, Grey Rabbit, I shall be back for supper, and mind there is something nice."

He stepped out of the little door into the sunshine.

"Take care of yourself," cried Grey Rabbit, running after him and waving her paw. "Give Toad our present."

"Don't forget to bring a present back," called Squirrel.

Hare was going to visit the famous Toad who lived in Ash Wood. Squirrel had laughed when he had told her he was going, and said, "You never dare."

"Daren't I?" he had said. "You'll see!"

Grey Rabbit decided to give the house a summer cleaning while he was away. So Squirrel took her knitting up an apple tree to be out of the way, and Little Grey Rabbit, with scrubbing brush and pail, started to clean the rooms.

Hare shut the garden gate with a bang, and prepared to leap over the brook.

But he changed his mind, and sat down by the water. A mocking voice cried, "Haven't you gone yet? You'll never get to Ash Wood if you don't start," and he saw Squirrel's face peering down from the apple tree.

Hare marched off, pretending not to hear.

Suddenly he bumped into a scared rabbit, who was walking along looking behind him. Both fell head over heels, but the rabbit picked himself up and scurried off.

Hare ran on until he came to a hollow oak tree with
a silver bell.

He rang the bell, and a sleepy voice called, "What do you
want, Hare?" Wise Owl looked out, blinking in the sunlight.

Hare faltered. "Er… which is the way to Ash Wood, please?"

Wise Owl looked down severely. "Where is your money?
I must be paid for helping you. I'll take those buttons from
your coat," he said, and he clambered down and cut them off.

"Go through the teasel field, through the village, across the railway, through Bilberry Wood, and Ash Wood is at the top of the hill," said Owl. "A fox lives in Bilberry Wood."

Hare turned pale. "I expect the fox won't notice me. I'm a pretty fast runner," he said.

He ran down the stony path to the gate at the end of the wood. In the teasel field were red butterflies, brown bumblebees, busy hoverflies, red-caped ladybirds, and field mice in bonnets and shawls running errands, strolling home, gossiping by the tiny green paths, and playing on swings and roundabouts.

Hare walked across the field swinging his stick, feeling very important in his bright coat among all these little people.

"Where are you going, stranger?" asked a brown rabbit.

"To Ash Wood, to visit Toad," answered Hare pompously.

"My, you are a traveller!" exclaimed the rabbit admiringly.

"I am that," said Hare.

"What other countries have you seen?" enquired the rabbit.

"Well… I've seen too many to tell you about. I'm a very famous Hare."

"Will you tell us about Ash Wood when you come back?" asked the animals.

"That I will, if you meet me at half-past twelve."

"There's a fox in Bilberry Wood," said a quiet little hedgehog.

"I'm not afraid of a fox!" cried Hare.

Then he lay down, put his two paws under his nose and fell asleep.

He was awakened by the youngest rabbit, who tugged at his watch. He sprang up in a hurry; he had slept longer than he intended.

Hare left the field by a gap in the hedge and ran through the village, then leaped the limestone wall and crossed the field to the railway. The roar of a train terrified him, and he scampered across and hid in the grass while the express rushed by.

"That's a dragon," he said. "I must be in China. I *shall* have some adventures to talk about when I get home."

He climbed up a steep path into a rocky wood.

"Can you tell me the time?" asked a silken voice, and Hare saw a fine gentleman in a red coat sitting on a fallen tree.

"Half-past twelve," said Hare, consulting his watch.

"Really? As early as that? Perhaps you would like to see my collection of birds' eggs?"

"Delighted," said Hare. "On my return. I am a bit of a collector myself. I collect noughts and crosses." And he trotted on, while the fine gentleman gazed longingly after him.

There was a curious musky smell that disturbed Hare. "It must be some foreign scent on the gentleman's handkerchief," he thought.

He picked up a branch of honeysuckle and twined it round his head, and held a sprig of marjoram to his nose, but the smell remained until he left the wood and crossed the fields to the farm on the ridge.

Dappled cows stood under the trees, and a score of hens chattered excitedly about the fox who, the night before, had tried to open the hen-house door.

In front of Hare lay Ash Wood. Apple-green moths and honeybees came to meet him as he entered. The flowers grew in groups: a patch of red campion here, a clump of forget-me-nots there, and tall bell-flowers in their blues and purples, like mists on the ground.

"Herbs for old Toad, I suppose," said Hare. "He does a lot of doctoring, they say."

In the middle of the wood was a bog, and there, perched on an island, was a small house with a roof thatched with rushes.

"Who's there?" boomed a voice.

"It's Hare, from Grey Rabbit's house over the valley."

The little door opened slowly and Toad waddled out, leaning

on a crutch. His eyes were bright as green lamps and his cheeks were wrinkled with age.

"I have brought a present," said Hare. He searched all his pockets, then took off his coat.

"Here it is!" he cried at last. "Grey Rabbit stitched it into my coat lining." He brought out an egg-beater.

"It's to beat eggs, you know, make them frothy," explained Hare.

Toad was entranced. He held it between his knees and turned the handle so the wheels whizzed.

"Come in, come in, Hare," he cried, throwing open the little door. Hare walked through to a courtyard with a fountain.

Toad rang a bell, and two frogs appeared.

"Bring refreshments," he commanded, "and a bowl of eggs."

The frogs returned with saffron cake, which Hare ate greedily. Then Toad beat up the eggs, and made wonderful drinks that astonished Hare.

"I have no teeth," Toad explained. "It's a most useful gift, most useful. I have never been so pleased."

He took Hare to a cupboard that was crammed with odds and ends.

"Choose a present for yourself, and one for each of your friends," said Toad.

Hare chose a tiny pair of slippers for Little Grey Rabbit, a box-wood flute for Squirrel, and a penknife with a corkscrew for himself.

Then Toad unlocked a secret drawer and took out a small bottle labelled 'Venom'.

"I shall give you a bottle of my famous venom," he said, "but take great care of it. You had better give it to Grey Rabbit to put in the medicine cupboard."

As Hare waded off through the bog he turned around and saw Toad busily beating the air with the egg-beater.

It was dusk when he ran across the fields to Bilberry Wood.

"Hello!" said a voice. "You've been a long time." Hare saw the red-coated gentleman sitting on a stile. At the same moment the strange musky odour came floating towards him, and his heart fluttered and bumped.

"Oh, sir!" said he. "You quite startled me. I had forgotten about you."

"Why, young fellow, I've been expecting you to supper," replied the fox with a leer.

"I'm afraid it's too late. I'll put off my visit, if you don't mind," said Hare.

"It's quite early, and really you *must* come. Everything is ready," said the fox.

They arrived at a ruined mill house. The fox pushed Hare into the kitchen. On the table was a very large dish, as big as Hare, a plate, a long cruel knife and a pot of redcurrant jelly.

Hare felt very uncomfortable. "I really must go."

"Not yet, not yet. You've only just come," said the fox. "Would you mind taking off your coat and waistcoat? They might fit a young friend of mine."

Hare grew more and more alarmed. He handed his lovely blue coat and waistcoat to the fox, and a paper fell out of the pocket.

"What's this?" asked the fox, and opened the paper, which was covered with noughts and crosses.

"It's a game," stammered Hare.

"Let us play," said the fox.

He learned quickly and beat Hare every time. Hare was too frightened to look what he was doing; his eyes were glancing round the room. The door was locked, and the broken window gave the only chance of escape.

The fox picked up Hare's coat and turned out the pockets. He brought out the venom bottle.

"What have we here?" he said. "Scent? Conceited Hare to carry scent in your pocket!"

He took out the cork and put it to his nose. His eyes closed, his ears drooped, and he sank his head onto the table, insensible.

Hare sprang up, seized the bottle of venom, swept up the slippers, his watch and the flute in his paw, and made for the window.

Away he ran through the wood, tumbling over stones, slipping, sliding and rolling down slopes.

He crossed the railway line and ran through the edge of the village, where dim lights shone in the windows.

When he arrived in the teasel field he found four sleepy little rabbits and a hedgehog, waiting for him.

"Here he comes, here he comes! Hurrah!" they cried. "What time is it? We've waited for ages."

"Half-past twelve," panted Hare, and he stopped a moment to breathe.

"You've been a very long time," said the hedgehog.

"I stopped to play noughts and crosses with Mr Fox," said Hare, and they all opened their mouths wide with astonishment. Then he hurried on.

"It's been wonderful to meet a real explorer," they said.

Hare clasped the bottle of venom in his paw as he went through the wood, ready for any weasel or stoat he might meet.

As he ran out of the trees he saw a candle burning in the window of the little house, and he shouted for joy.

Grey Rabbit and Squirrel heard him and came running down the path.

"Oh Hare, we thought you were dead, especially as Wise Owl told us there was a fox in Bilberry Wood."

"He caught me," confessed Hare, "and I only escaped through Toad's present to us all."

They entered the house and Hare told his story, and put his presents on the table. Squirrel tootled on the flute, and Grey Rabbit tried on the slippers, which fitted perfectly. The venom she locked up in the medicine cupboard.

"I've had my great adventure," said Hare. "I am famous all over the world, and now I shall lead a quiet life at the fireside." He wound up his watch, took his candle and went upstairs to bed.

Grey Rabbit and Squirrel looked at one another and laughed softly. Then they followed, and soon the only sounds in the house were the snores of Columbus Hare.

The End

It is Fuzzypeg the Hedgehog's birthday.
He is one year old – nearly grown up – and is finally
allowed out on his own. But his mother warns him to be careful,
because there are dangers about. When Fuzzypeg gets into
trouble and doesn't come home, Little Grey Rabbit and her
friends gather together and do all in their power to rescue him.

THE STORY OF
FUZZYPEG
THE HEDGEHOG

EARLY ONE SUMMER MORNING, when the white mist lay
over the fields like a soft blanket, old Milkman Hedgehog
uncurled himself and rolled out of bed.

"Don't wake Fuzzypeg," called Mrs Hedgehog, as he
struggled with a sheet that was all mixed up in his prickles.

He stooped over Fuzzypeg, who lay curled up in bed,
a small ball of spikes.

"He'll be a grand fellow when he is grown up," he said
to his wife.

Hedgehog went downstairs with his prickles lowered, lest
they should brush the whitewash off the ceiling, and walked

into the kitchen. Mrs Hedgehog polished him up with a duster and gave him a clean brown handkerchief.

He opened the door and took down from a branch a small wooden yoke, which he slung across his shoulders. From it he hung two little wooden pails, then he started off to get the milk.

"Don't be late," called Mrs Hedgehog. "Breakfast is at six o'clock today. It is Fuzzypeg's birthday."

He walked through the meadow and under the five-barred gate. Out of the whiteness appeared a herd of cows.

"Coo-up," called Hedgehog, and a cow raised her head and watched him unhook his pails. "Lie down," he commanded, and she obediently lay down.

Hedgehog milked steadily until the little pails were frothing over. He politely thanked the cow and set off to the house where Little Grey Rabbit lived with her friends Hare and Squirrel.

"You're early, Hedgehog," said Grey Rabbit as she opened the door.

"Yes, Grey Rabbit, it is my little Fuzzypeg's birthday," replied Hedgehog. "He is a year old – half grown up."

"Wait a minute, and I will send him a present." She disappeared inside and came back with a hen's egg.

"It's a boiled egg," she said. "Fuzzypeg can play ball with it."

Hedgehog thanked her and carried on to Moldy Warp the Mole's house. Moldy Warp gave him another present for Fuzzypeg.

"It's a scrambled egg," he said. "I had to scramble under a haystack to find it."

Hedgehog walked across the field to an old black house where Rat lived. He felt slightly nervous at Rat's house, although Rat seemed a friendly fellow.

"Here's the milk," said Hedgehog quickly.

"You're in a hurry," said Rat.

"It's my Fuzzypeg's birthday."

"I will send him a present," said Rat. He ran to his cupboard and took out an egg. "It's a poached egg," he said. "I poached it from the hen-house."

Next, Hedgehog set off for Red Squirrel's house, where he received another present for Fuzzypeg.

"It's an old-laid egg," said Red Squirrel, "the same age as Fuzzypeg."

"How kind everyone is!" thought Hedgehog as he hurried home.

Fuzzypeg was sitting on a little chair waiting for his bread and milk when Hedgehog arrived. He had the scrambled egg for breakfast, and divided the poached egg between his father and mother.

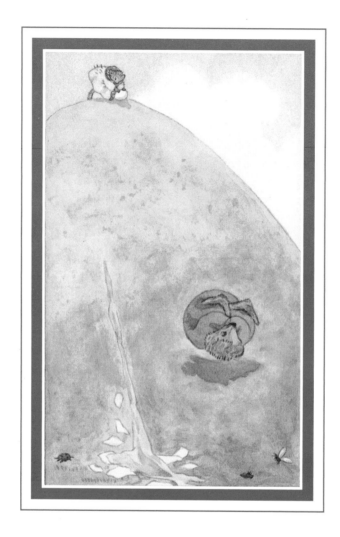

After breakfast, Hedgehog and Fuzzypeg went out to play 'Rolling'. They climbed a hill with the old-laid egg and the boiled egg, and they all rolled down to the bottom.

Bumpity-bump went Fuzzypeg. *Bumpity-bump* went the boiled egg. *Squishity-squash* went the old-laid egg.

Such a smell came from the broken egg! Hedgehog and
Fuzzypeg took to their heels and ran all the way home.

When evening came, Hedgehog gave Fuzzypeg his present.
He opened it with trembling paws to find a little white cage.

Inside were two small creatures that sent out a beautiful soft
light, so the cage was like a fairy lantern in the twilight.

"What are they?" asked Fuzzypeg.

"Glow-worms," replied Hedgehog. "Two tame glow-worms.
Feed them and treat them kindly and then you can let them
loose in the hedge-garden."

One day soon after, Fuzzypeg and Hedgehog were strolling near the farm when suddenly the hens began to cry and hiss and scream.

All of the hens rushed to the shelter of the farm – all except Speckledy Hen, who was too frightened to move. She stood staring at an adder, which glided nearer and nearer.

Hedgehog sprang at the adder's tail, holding it tight. The adder tried to bite him over and over again, but Hedgehog never let go until the adder lay dead.

"It's months since I tasted Hadder Pie," he said as he slung the adder across his back and went home with the admiring Fuzzypeg.

After a fine dinner of adder pie, Fuzzypeg ran out to play with his cousins, Tim and Bill Hedgehog.

"My father killed a Nadder!" he said. "He held its tail till it was dead!"

"That's nothing," said Bill scornfully. "My father pounced on a lion's tail and held it till it was dead."

Fuzzypeg walked home with a heavy heart.

"Mother," he said, "could my father pounce on a lion and hold its tail till it was dead?"

"Of course he could," replied Mrs Hedgehog, looking up from her sewing.

"He could fight an elephant, I expect," thought Fuzzypeg.

The next day, Mrs Hedgehog made a hay-seed cake.

"Take this to Speckledy Hen," she said to Fuzzypeg. "Do not dawdle on the way home. Walk on the little green path, not on the broad white road. There are dangers about – weasels, stoats, snakes and worse."

"What do I do if I meet a Danger?" asked Fuzzypeg.

"Roll up in a ball, and keep your face hidden."

"Suppose I meet a lion?"

"You won't meet a lion," she laughed.

Fuzzypeg trotted through the fields until he met Speckledy Hen.

"Mother sent you a hay-seed cake," he said.

"How sweet it smells!" said the hen. "Now come with me and I will show you where the finest acorns fall."

By the time Fuzzypeg started home it was getting late. He hadn't gone far when he saw Hare sitting on a grassy bank.

"Stop and play a minute," said Hare. Fuzzypeg stopped a minute, and a minute more, while Hare tried to explain noughts and crosses to him.

At last, Fuzzypeg hurried home, thinking of his supper.

Suddenly he saw a big, white, curly-haired animal. It sprang towards him.

"A lion!" he thought, and rolled into a ball.

"Woof, woof!" roared the lion.

"Good dog," said a voice.

Fuzzypeg was picked up and carried away.

"You let me go!" he squeaked. "My father once killed a lion!"

He was put down on a path in a garden, where he uncurled and bolted for the gate. But he was not quick enough, for an enormous flowerpot was placed on top of him.

"I'll bring you some bread and milk," said the voice, then it went away, and Fuzzypeg was alone in the dark.

When no little hedgehog came home, old Hedgehog went to look for him. He found a piece of paper covered with Os and Xs. A little further on he found a bundle of acorns tied in a tiny handkerchief, and a pair of red shoes.

He was in despair as he set off for Grey Rabbit's house. He knocked at the door, and Squirrel answered.

"No milk tonight, thank you," she said, shutting the door.

"Please ma'am, it's my little Fuzzypeg. He's lost."

"Does anyone know where Fuzzypeg is?" Squirrel called into the house. Little Grey Rabbit and Hare came running.

"I've seen him," said Hare. "We had a game of noughts and crosses."

Hedgehog took the paper from his pocket.

"Yes, that's it," said Hare.

"What happened then?" asked Hedgehog.

"He ran on and on, and I ran the other way."

"I am so sorry, Hedgehog," said Grey Rabbit. "I think you should ask Wise Owl for help."

"Oh no," said Hedgehog, "he might be hungry."

"If you wave a white handkerchief for a truce, you will be safe."

Little Grey Rabbit tied a handkerchief to his prickles, and he set off into the wood.

Hedgehog reached Wise Owl's oak tree and rang the silvery bell.

"What do you want?" called Owl.

"I've lost my Fuzzypeg, and Grey Rabbit thought you could find him."

Wise Owl was flattered. "Perhaps I can, but you must bring me a quill for a pen, a can of milk and a new-laid egg. Bring them at dawn, and you shall have news of your son."

Wise Owl flew over the fields looking for Fuzzypeg, but couldn't see him anywhere.

"Stoat, have you seen little Hedgehog?" he asked a shifty-eyed fellow, creeping along the hedges.

"No sir," said Stoat. "I wish I had seen him," he muttered, when Owl had flown away.

"Yard dog, have you seen little Hedgehog?" Owl asked
a curly white dog sitting outside a kennel.

"Yes," said the dog, "but I shall tell you nothing about him.
I belong to the house, and you belong to the wood."

"He must be near," thought Owl.
As he flew slowly over the garden, he heard a soft sobbing sound
coming from a large flowerpot. He flew down and looked
through the hole in the top.

"Is that you, little Hedgehog?" he asked.

"Yes, it's me," cried Fuzzypeg, trembling.

"Help is coming!" said Wise Owl, and flew away home.

At dawn, Hedgehog came to Wise Owl's house with a can of milk, a goose-quill for a pen and a new-laid egg.

"Put them down there, Hedgehog," said Owl. "Your son is safe under a flowerpot in the farmer's garden."

Hedgehog thanked him and started home at a run, calling on his way for Little Grey Rabbit, Hare, Squirrel and Moldy Warp. Mrs Hedgehog ran to the door when she heard the patter of little feet, and joined them.

They all ran through the fields, Hare and Little Grey Rabbit leading, Squirrel coming next, Hedgehog and Mrs Hedgehog panting after… and Moldy Warp far behind.

They squeezed under the gate (except for fat Hare, who had to climb the wall), and ran down the little path to the enormous plant pot.

"Are you there, Fuzzypeg?" called old Hedgehog.

"Yes, Father, are you?" answered a small, faint voice.

"Yes, we are all here," said Hedgehog; "Squirrel, Hare and Grey Rabbit, and Moldy Warp is on the way."

He turned to the animals. "All push, and over the plant pot must go."

So they pushed and they pushed, but the pot didn't move.

"All together! Shove!" called Hedgehog, but still the pot didn't move.

Just then, Rat strolled up. "What are you doing?" he asked.

"Fuzzypeg is under this plant pot," explained Hedgehog.

"But you will never move that thing if Hare pushes one way and you all push the other. Now heave!" shouted Rat, but the plant pot still didn't move.

Then Moldy Warp arrived.

"This is the way," he said. And he began to dig. Earth flew up in a shower, and soon Moldy Warp had disappeared down the tunnel. The animals waited.

Then a tiny snout appeared, and little Fuzzypeg crawled up

the tunnel to be hugged, prickles and all, by Hedgehog and his wife.

A minute later came Mole, wiping his lips.

"I stopped to finish his bread and milk," he explained. "It was a pity to waste them."

He rammed the soil back down the tunnel and the happy procession started home.

"Come into the garden and have some refreshments," said Mrs Hedgehog when they got back. There were egg sandwiches, acorns baked in their skins, rose-hip jam, fresh blackberries and cream, mushrooms on toast and crab-apple cider.

When Hare, Squirrel and Little Grey Rabbit went home, they each took a small quill pen, which the grateful Hedgehog had made for them; but Moldy Warp wouldn't accept anything. He said that digging was more in his line than writing, and anyway, he already had everything he wanted in his castle under the Ten-Acre Field.

The End

ONE COLD DAY, *when even the brook is frozen,*
Little Grey Rabbit, Squirrel and Hare decide to go skating.
But when they return from their fun day on the ice,
they find an unwelcome guest tucked up in Squirrel's bed.
And so they decide to teach the visitor a lesson
that gets him into a bit of a twist…

SQUIRREL
GOES SKATING

EVERYTHING WAS FROZEN. Even the brook, which ran past Little Grey Rabbit's house on the edge of the wood, was thick with ice. Each blade of grass had a white fringe, and the black, leafless trees were patterned with shining crystals.

On every window of the house were Jack Frost's pictures – trees and ferns and flowers in silver.

Little Grey Rabbit stood looking at them, when Hare came downstairs in his brown dressing gown.

"Grey Rabbit! Grey Rabbit!" he called. "Put some more wood on the fire. It's bitter cold today."

Grey Rabbit left the window and put a log on the fire.

"I believe I've got a chilblain," said Hare in a complaining voice, rubbing his sore toe. "Yes I thought so. It's a big chilblain! What can you do for it, Grey Rabbit?"

Grey Rabbit went to the medicine cupboard and looked at the bottles which stood in a row.

There was Primrose wine for coughs and colds and feast days. There was Dandelion for toothache, and Dock leaves for bruises, St. John's wort for cuts, but nothing for chilblains.

"There isn't anything for chilblains," said Grey Rabbit, sadly.

"Ow! Ow!" exclaimed Hare, rubbing his toe again. "Do think of something, Grey Rabbit. You don't know how it hurts!"

"Moldy Warp once told me to use snow," said Grey Rabbit. "I'll get some."

She ran outside and scraped the frost from the grass. Then she rubbed Hare's foot till the chilblain disappeared.

"Grey Rabbit! Grey Rabbit!" called Squirrel, coming downstairs with a shawl over her shoulders. "Pile up the fire and keep out the cold. You've had the door open this frosty morning."

So Grey Rabbit put another log on the fire, and sent away the little wind which had rushed in when she went out.

At last they sat down to breakfast, with hot tea and thick buttered toast.

"Milk-o," called a voice, and Hedgehog knocked at the door.

"It's fruz today," said he, as he turned a solid lump of milk out of his can.

"I went to the cow-house – it's the only really warm place on a day like this – but icicles hung all round my little door, and nearly stabbed me as I went in."

He was indeed a strange sight, with his prickles all frost-covered.

"Come in and warm yourself," said Grey Rabbit.

He stamped his feet at the door and tiptoed over to the fire. Grey Rabbit gave him a cup of tea. And between sips from the saucer, he talked.

"There's skating over Tom Tiddler's Way, and I've heard tell everyone is going," he said.

"Moldy Warp was trying on his skates as I came past, and I met a couple of brown rabbits with their toboggan."

Hare put down his cup.

"Let's go too," said he. "Hurry up everybody," and he gobbled up his breakfast as fast as he could.

"There's no hurry, Mr Hare," drawled Hedgehog. "Ice'll wait. There'll be no thaw this side of Christmas, I can tell 'ee that." And he took another sip of his tea.

"Well, I must be getting on," he said, wiping his mouth with his red handkerchief. And he tiptoed out again, leaving a little stream of icy water on the floor. Grey Rabbit wiped it away.

Hare jumped up from the table. "Have you ever seen me skate?" he asked. "I'm a very good skater. Did you ever hear how I skated round the lily pond backwards? I'll tell you about it."

"Not now," said Grey Rabbit. "We must get our skates cleaned, and the house tidied and the lunch ready."

"And put on our best clothes," added Squirrel.

Hare went out to clean the skates, Squirrel disappeared upstairs, and Grey Rabbit did everything else as quickly as she could. She swept the floor, made up the fire, cut the sandwiches and packed them in the basket. She even remembered to put in an extra loaf for any hungry rooks who might be on the ice.

When she stood ready to go, with a little red muffler round her neck, she called Hare and Squirrel.

"Hare, are you ready? Hare?"

Hare came running with a basket of icicles. "I've been collecting these to take for drinks," he said. "You just suck one, like this."

"That's splendid," said Grey Rabbit, "but I think we should take the kettle too, for hot drinks."

"And a lemon," added Hare, "for hot lemonade."

"But you haven't changed out of your dressing gown," said Grey Rabbit. "And where are the skates?"

"Oh, Jemima!" exclaimed Hare. "I forgot about the skates and my dressing gown."

He hurried off to get ready.

"Squirrel! Squirrel! Are you ready? We're going," called Grey Rabbit at the foot of the stairs.

"Coming," called Squirrel, and Grey Rabbit took a last look round. The table was laid for their return, when they would be tired and hungry. There was herb-pie, an apple tart, and nut cutlets. "I'll put out a bottle of Primrose wine," she said, going to the larder.

"Can you come here?" called Squirrel in a muffled voice. Grey Rabbit and Hare both hurried upstairs. In Squirrel's room a green dress was jumping about with two little paws waving in the air. A green ribboned tail stuck half-out of the neck of the dress, and Squirrel's head couldn't find a way out at all.

Hare and Grey Rabbit sank down on the bed, helpless with laughter. When at last they straightened her out they found Squirrel had decked herself with green bows and hung a locket round her neck.

Off they went at last, Grey Rabbit carrying the basket of food, Hare swinging the basket of icicles in one paw and the kettle in the other, and Squirrel following with the skates dangling on her arms.

They locked the door and put the key on the window sill. Over it they sprinkled leaves and grass and a few icicles.

Then the three animals ran down the lane and across the fields towards Tom Tiddler's Way.

Little hurrying footsteps came along a side path, and a party of brown rabbits, each with a pair of skates, joined them.

Hare led the way, past Moldy Warp's house, and through the fields where Grey Rabbit had picked primroses for wine in the spring.

"Stop a minute," called a voice as they crossed a frozen stream and handsome Water-rat joined them.

At last they reached the pond, which lay in the centre of a small field. Already many animals were on the ice, and the air was filled with merry cries. The newcomers sat down and put on their skates. Grey Rabbit placed her basket of food in the care of Mrs Hedgehog, who sat on a log, watching her son, Fuzzypeg.

Soon they were laughing and shouting with the others, as they skimmed over the ice.

Hare tried to do the outside edge, and got mixed up with the skates of a white duck. He fell down with a thump and bruised his forehead.

"Grey Rabbit! Grey Rabbit!" he called. "Grey Rabbit! I've bumped myself." And Grey Rabbit ran up and rubbed him with her paw. She dusted the powdered snow off his coat, and helped him to his unsteady feet. Then she went to some young brown rabbits who were in difficulties. Every time they started off, one of them sat down, and tumbled into the others, so that they were a continual bunch of kicking legs.

Grey Rabbit and Water-rat linked paws with the young rabbits and steered them across the pond, to their joy and happiness. Away they went, ears back, heads up, fur stiff in the wind, their eyes shining and their breath coming and going in little puffs, as their tiny feet glided over the ice.

"I'm hungry," called Hare. "Let's have lunch." So they returned to Mrs Hedgehog, who still sat with her eyes on young Fuzzypeg and on no one else. Grey Rabbit unpacked the basket of food, and Squirrel invited Water-rat, Moldy Warp, Mrs Hedgehog and Fuzzypeg to join them.

There was enough for all, and still there was a loaf left for the hungry black-coated rooks who loitered on the pond's edge.

Hare's icicles were very thin by now, but he handed round the basket and each sucked the sweet cold ice. The rooks collected sticks for a fire, and soon Grey Rabbit had a kettle boiling and hot drinks of lemonade for everyone.

"Sour! Sour!" grimaced little Fuzzypeg, but his mother nudged him to remember his manners.

They all returned to the ice and skated until the red sun set behind the hills. Dark shadows spread across the fields as the animals removed their skates and set off home.

"It *has* been a jolly day," said Grey Rabbit to Water-rat and Moldy Warp. "Goodbye. Perhaps we will come again tomorrow."

"Goodnight. Goodnight," resounded round the pond.

"Did you see me skate?" asked Hare, excitedly. "I did the double-outside-edge backwards."

"I saw all the little rabbits and field mice you knocked down," said Squirrel severely.

"Hush!" said Grey Rabbit. "Don't make a noise. Wise Owl doesn't like it."

The key was on the window sill under the pile of grass but there were footprints in the garden.

"Someone's been here while we've been skating," said Squirrel, looking anxiously up and down.

They all hurried inside and stared in dismay. On the table lay the remains of the feast, only dirty dishes, and crusts, and an empty bottle of Primrose wine.

"Oh! Oh!" cried Hare. "I was so hungry."

"Oh! Oh!" cried Squirrel. "I was so thirsty."

"Oh! Oh!" cried Grey Rabbit. "I left such a feast and now look at it."

"Who's been here since we've been gone?" they said, running to the larder.

Not a scrap of food remained. Everything was gone and all over the floor were footprints.

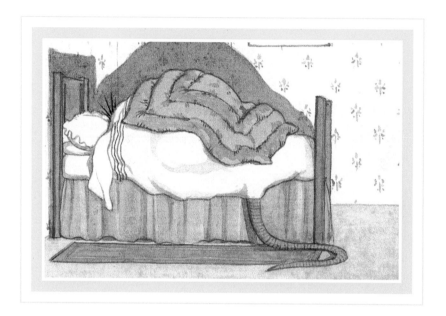

They ran upstairs to the bedrooms, each carrying a candlestick.

"There's no one in my attic," whispered Grey Rabbit, as she peeped in.

"And there's no one in my room," said Hare, picking up his dressing gown from the floor where he had flung it.

"Oo-Oo-Oo," squeaked Squirrel. "Somebody's sleeping in *my* bed! Oo-Oo-Oo."

They peered through the door, but all they could see was a long thin tail hanging down on the floor, and long black whiskers sticking out of the sheets.

"Who is it?" whispered Squirrel in a trembling voice.

"It's Rat's tail," said Hare.

"They're Rat's whiskers," said Grey Rabbit, below her breath.

"Then it must be Rat himself," sobbed Squirrel.

They tiptoed downstairs, each with a candle dripping wax on the steps, they were so alarmed.

"What shall we do?" they asked each other as they stood in the untidy kitchen.

Hare trembled so much that the candle fell out and burned his paws.

Squirrel forgot to use her handkerchief in her agitation and wiped her streaming eyes on her ribboned tail.

Grey Rabbit shivered as she thought of Rat's sharp teeth. But no sound came from the bedroom except snores.

"He must get out of my bed," said Squirrel. "We must shoo him out."

"But he ought to be punished," said Grey Rabbit. "We ought to make him remember his wickedness."

"When I want to remember anything I tie a knot in my handkerchief," said Hare.

Then Squirrel spoke these astonishing words: "I can tie knots," said she. "I will tie a knot in Rat's tail, and it will never, never come undone. Then he will never, never forget his wickedness."

Squirrel crept upstairs again, and Hare and Grey Rabbit followed, each with a candle to light up her task.

Squirrel picked up the long tail and tied it, and twisted it, and turned it, and doubled it, and looped it till it made one great knot, and Rat never awoke, for he had eaten and drunk so much from Little Grey Rabbit's larder.

They shut the door and ran downstairs, with beating hearts.

"Now we must frighten him away," said Grey Rabbit.

Hare took the tongs and poker, Grey Rabbit took two saucepan lids, and Squirrel took the bundle of skates. They hammered and banged against the bedroom door and made such a clang and clatter, such a rattle and racket that Rat awoke.

He sprang out of bed, opened the window and jumped out.

"Whatever's that a-bumping and a-clumping behind me?" said he to himself, and he turned round to find his tail in a knot.

He ran down the paths with the knot reminding him of his wickedness all the way, and he didn't like it at all.

At last he sat down and tried to undo the knot, but just then Wise Owl came sailing along the sky. He spied Rat down below, trying to unfasten his tail.

"Hello, Rat!" said he, and he flew down to look. "Hello! Been in mischief?" He chuckled in a goblin way, which made Rat shiver, then flew soundlessly away.

In the little house Grey Rabbit put clean sheets on Squirrel's bed, Squirrel swept the floor and Hare made a fire in the kitchen to cheer everybody up as there was no food.

Suddenly there came a knock at the door.

Thump! thump! thump!

The three animals looked at one another anxiously.

"Grey Rabbit! Open the door," cried a voice.

"That's Moldy Warp," said Grey Rabbit, and she flung wide the door.

"We are so glad to see you," she cried, as the mole staggered in with a big hamper, followed by Water-rat with another.

They opened the baskets and took out eggs, sandwiches, teacakes, a Bakewell tart, and a big plum-cake with icing.

"Hurrah!" cried Little Grey Rabbit, Squirrel and Hare.

"Hedgehog is bringing an extra can of milk," said the mole. "I thought you might be short. Somebody whispered that you had a visitor today."

"It's still fruz," said old Hedgehog, putting the milk on the table.

"Come along, Hedgehog, and join the party," they cried, and he sat down on the settle, keeping his prickles to himself.

After supper they sang songs, ending up with, "He's a jolly good fellow," and toasted Moldy Warp and Water-rat with a bottle of Primrose wine which Rat had overlooked.

Then Mole, Water-rat, and Hedgehog said goodbye, and walked along the quiet field paths to their homes.

The End

*As Christmas gets closer, the woodland animals
are busily preparing for the magical day. When Little Grey
Rabbit goes to the market, she returns with a truly special gift
for Squirrel and Hare. But when Hare loses it in the snow,
will the three friends ever see their lovely present again?*

LITTLE GREY RABBIT'S
CHRISTMAS

IT HAD BEEN SNOWING FOR HOURS. Hare stood in the garden of the little house at the end of the wood, watching the snowflakes tumbling down like white feathers from the grey sky.

"Whatever are you doing, Hare?" cried Squirrel, who was sitting close to the fire. "Come in! You'll catch cold."

"I am catching cold, and eating it too," replied Hare, happily.

"Hare! How long do you think Grey Rabbit will be? Can you see her coming? What is she doing?" called Squirrel again.

"She's at the market, buying a Christmas feast for all of us,"

replied Hare, and he caught an extra large snowflake on his red tongue.

As he spoke, a small stout animal came trudging up the lane, laden with a heavy basket and a string bag bulging with knobbly surprises. Straggling behind was a little snow-covered creature.

"There she is!" cried Hare, leaping forward. "Make the tea, Squirrel."

He ran down the path, and then stopped, disappointed. "It's only Mrs Hedgehog!" he muttered. "And Fuzzypeg," he added, as he recognised the little fellow.

"Have you seen Little Grey Rabbit?" asked Hare, as he leaned over the gate.

"I have indeed," said Mrs Hedgehog, resting her burden on the snow. "She was at the market along of me. Then she went to talk to Old Joe the carpenter."

"What did she want with Joe?" asked Hare.

"Please Sir!" cried Fuzzypeg. "I knows, Sir. I knows what Grey Rabbit went to the carpenter for."

"Sh-sh!" Mrs Hedgehog shook her head at her son. "You mustn't let the cat out of the bag." Then, picking up her basket, she continued on her way, with little Fuzzypeg protesting: "There wasn't a cat in the bag, Mother. There wasn't."

It was growing dark when Squirrel and Hare heard the sound of merry voices and the ringing of bells.

They ran to the door, and what should they see but a fine scarlet sledge drawn by two young rabbits, with Little Grey Rabbit herself sitting cosily on the top!

"Oh Grey Rabbit, what a lovely sledge!" cried Squirrel, and she rubbed her paws over the smooth sides.

"Grey Rabbit! Our names are on it!" shouted Hare.

He pointed excitedly to the words, 'Squirrel, Hare and Little Grey Rabbit' written round the sides. "It's ours. It says so!"

"Yes. It is our very own," said Grey Rabbit. "I ordered it from Old Joe, and these kind rabbits insisted on bringing me home."

After breakfast the next day, Squirrel and Grey Rabbit sat on the sledge, and Hare pulled them over the field.

They came to their favourite hill. Hare mounted behind them, and stretched out his long legs.

"One to be ready!

"Two to be steady!

"Three to be off!" he cried, and away they went down the steep slope.

"Whoo-oo-oo!" cried Hare. "What a speed! Whoops! Whoa!"

But the sledge wouldn't stop.

At last it struck a mole-hill, and over they all toppled, head over heels.

"Sixty miles an hour!" cried Hare, sitting up and rubbing his elbow.

Little Fuzzypeg, carrying a slice of bread and jam, came to watch the fun. He stared at the three dragging their sledge up the slope.

"I want to toboggan," he said softly, but nobody heard. "Look at *me* toboggan! Watch *me*!" cried Fuzzypeg. He made himself into a ball and rolled down the hill, faster and faster. When he got to the bottom there was no Fuzzypeg to be seen, only an enormous snowball.

"What a big snowball!" cried Squirrel, climbing off the sledge.

"What a beauty!" exclaimed Grey Rabbit.

"Help! Help!" squeaked a tiny voice. "Get me out!"

"What's that?" cried Squirrel.

"Help! Help!" piped Fuzzypeg.

"That's a talking snowball," said Hare. "Isn't that interesting? I shall take it home and keep it in the garden."

He dragged the large ball on to the sledge and pulled the load uphill. When he reached the top, Hare rolled the ball to the ground and gave it a kick.

"Ugh!" he cried, limping. "There's a thorn inside."

"Help! Help!" shrieked the tiny faraway voice. "Lemme out!"

"That sounds like Fuzzypeg," said Grey Rabbit, and she bent over and loosened the caked snow.

Out came the little hedgehog, eating his bread and jam.

"However did you get inside a snowball?" asked Hare.

"I didn't get inside. It got round me," replied Fuzzypeg. "Can I go on your sledge now?"

Hare took the little hedgehog for a ride, but when Fuzzypeg flung his arms round Hare's waist, he sprang shrieking away.

"That's enough," he said. "My motto is, 'Never go hedging with a sledgehog'. I mean to say, 'Never go sledging with a hedgehog'."

Fuzzypeg ran home and returned with a tea tray. After him came a crowd of rabbits, each carrying a tray, and they all rode helter-skelter down the slope, shouting and laughing as they tried to race each other.

Squirrel, Hare and Little Grey Rabbit took their sledge to Moldy Warp's house. Squirrel ran up the holly trees and gathered sprigs of the blazing red berries. The mole came out and showed them the mistletoe growing on an oak tree. And then he helped them to tie their branches on the sledge.

They said goodbye and hurried home.

Hare shut the sledge in the woodshed and carried the holly and mistletoe indoors. Grey Rabbit stood at the table making mince pies, while Hare and Squirrel decorated the room. They popped sprigs on the clock, over the corner cupboard, round the warming pan and on the dresser.

Little Grey Rabbit looked up from her patty-pans and waved her rolling pin to direct operations.

Up the lane came a little group, carrying rolls of music and pipes of straw. They talked softly as they walked up to the closed door of Grey Rabbit's house. They arranged themselves in a circle, they coughed and cleared their throats and held up their music to the moonlight.

"Now then, altogether!" cried an important-looking rabbit, playing a note on his straw pipe. "One, two, three!" and with their noses in the air they began to sing in small squeaky voices this Christmas carol:

"Holly red and mistletoe white,
The stars are shining with golden light,
Burning like candles this Holy Night,
Holly red and mistletoe white."

"Hush! What's that noise?" cried Hare, dropping his mistletoe.

"It's carollers!" said Grey Rabbit, and she held up her wooden spoon.

They flung wide the door and saw the little group of rabbits and hedgehogs, peering at their sheets of music.

"Come in! Come in!" cried Grey Rabbit. "Come and sing by the fireside. You look frozen with the cold."

"We're all right," said a big rabbit, "but a warm drink would wet our whistles."

Grey Rabbit took the two-handled Christmas mug of Primrose wine from the fire, and the carollers passed it round.

Then they stood by the hearth and sang all the songs they knew: "The moon shines bright", "I saw three ships a-sailing", and "Green grows the holly".

"Now we must be off," they said, when Grey Rabbit had given them hot mince pies. "We have to sing at all the rabbit houses tonight. Goodnight. Happy Christmas!"

Squirrel, Hare and Little Grey Rabbit stood watching the carollers as they crossed the fields, listening to "Holly red and mistletoe white", which the animals sang as they trotted along.

"I think I shall take the sledge and toboggan down the hill by moonlight," said Hare.

He seized the cord of the sledge and ran across the fields, and up the hill.

Then down he swooped, flying like a bird.

Again and again he rushed down, his eyes on the lovely moon. Suddenly he noticed a dark shadow running alongside. It was his own shadow, but Hare saw the long ears of a monster.

"Oh dear! Oh dear! Who is that fellow racing by my side?" he cried.

He took to his heels and hurried home, leaving the sledge lying in the field.

"Did you come without the sledge?" asked Squirrel. "Hare, you are a coward! I don't believe there was anybody at all.

"You ran away from your shadow. You've lost our lovely sledge!"

"Better than losing my lovely life," retorted Hare. He felt rather miserable. "I suppose we had better go to bed," he muttered. "I don't suppose there will be any presents tomorrow. I don't think Santa Claus will find this house with so much snow about!"

He went upstairs gloomily, but he hung up his furry stocking all the same, and so did Squirrel.

When all was quiet Grey Rabbit slipped out of bed. Under her bed was a store of parcels.

She opened them and filled the stockings with sugar-plums and lollipops. Then she ran downstairs to the kitchen, where the dying fire flickered softly.

She tied together sprays of holly and made a round ball called a Kissing Bunch. Then she hung it from a hook in the ceiling.

On Christmas morning Grey Rabbit was so sleepy she didn't wake up till Hare burst into her room.

"Grey Rabbit! Merry Christmas! He's been! Wake up! He's been in the night!"

"Who?" cried Grey Rabbit.

"Santa Claus!" cried Hare. "Quick! Come downstairs and see."

Grey Rabbit dressed hurriedly and entered the kitchen.

"Look at the Kissing Bunch!" said Hare. "Isn't it lovely! Let's all kiss under it."

So they gave their Christmas morning kisses under the round Christmas Bunch.

Robin the postman flew to the door with some Christmas cards and a letter. The little bird rested and ate some breakfast while Hare examined the letter.

"It's from Moldy Warp," he said.

"Yes, I know," replied Robin. "He gave it to me."

"You're reading it upside down, Hare!" cried Squirrel. She took the little letter and read, "Come tonight. Love from Moldy Warp."

"It's a party!" cried Hare. "Quick, Grey Rabbit! Write and say we'll come."

Grey Rabbit sat at her desk and wrote on an ivy leaf, "Thank you dear Moldy Warp."

Then away flew Robin with the leaf in his bag.

All day they enjoyed themselves, playing musical chairs, pulling tiny crackers, crunching lollipops.

They all trooped to the hill to look for the sledge, but it wasn't there. Snow had covered all traces of footprints.

"Santa Claus has borrowed it," said Grey Rabbit. "When the snow melts we shall find it."

When the first star appeared in the sky, the three animals wrapped themselves up in warm clothes, and set off for Moldy Warp's house. They carried presents for the lonely mole, and some of their own Christmas feast.

"What a pity you lost our sledge. We could have ridden on it tonight," said Squirrel to Hare.

When the three got near Moldy Warp's house they saw something glittering. A lighted tree grew by the path.

"Oh dear! Something's on fire!" cried Hare. "Let's put it out."

"Hush!" whispered Grey Rabbit. "It's a magical tree."

On every branch of the tree, candles wavered their tongues of flame. On the ground under the branches were bowls of hazel nuts, round loaves of bread, piles of cakes, small sacks of corn. There were jars of honey as big as thimbles, and bottles of heather ale.

"What do you think of my tree?" asked Moldy Warp, stepping out of the shadows.

"Is it a fairy tree?" asked Grey Rabbit.

"It's a Christmas tree," replied the mole. "It's for all the birds and beasts of the woods and fields. Now sit quietly and watch."

Across the snowy fields padded little creatures, all filled with curiosity to see the glowing tree.

"Help yourselves," cried Moldy Warp, waving his short arms. "It's Christmas. Eat and drink and warm yourselves."

From behind a tree Rat sidled towards Grey Rabbit.

"Miss Grey Rabbit," said he. "I found a scarlet sledge in the field last night, and as your family name was on it, I took the liberty of bringing it here."

"Oh, thank you, kind Rat," cried Grey Rabbit, clapping her paws. "The sledge is found! Come Hare! Squirrel! Moldy Warp!"

The scarlet sledge was clean and bright and on the top was a fleecy shawl. From under it Grey Rabbit drew three objects. The first was a walking stick made of holly wood. The second was a little wooden spoon. The third was a tiny box, and when Grey Rabbit opened the lid there was a little thimble inside which exactly fitted her.

"I've never had a thimble since Wise Owl swallowed mine," she said happily.

"Good Santa Claus," cried Hare. "He knew what we wanted."

"Only one person could make such delicate carvings," said Grey Rabbit.

"And that is Rat," said Squirrel.

"Three cheers for Rat!" cried Fuzzypeg, and they all cheered, "Hip! Hip! Hooray!"

Squirrel and Grey Rabbit climbed on the sledge, and Hare drew them over the snow.

"Goodnight. A happy Christmas!" they called.

"The same to you," answered Moldy Warp. The Hedgehog family waved and shouted, "Merry Christmas!"

"Heigh-ho! I'm sleepy," murmured Squirrel, "but it has been lovely. Thank you everyone for a happy day."

She curled down under the fleecy shawl by Grey Rabbit's side, clutching her wooden spoon. Grey Rabbit sat wide awake, her thimble was on her finger, her eyes shone with happiness.

Hare ran swiftly over the frozen snow, drawing the scarlet sledge towards the little house at the end of the wood.

"Mistletoe white and holly red,
The day is over, we're off to bed,
Tired body and sleepy head,
Mistletoe white and holly red."

The End

Little Grey Rabbit Quiz...

*How much can you remember from the
Little Grey Rabbit stories in this treasury?
Test your knowledge and then check your
answers on the very last page of this book.*

THE SQUIRREL, THE HARE AND THE LITTLE GREY RABBIT

1. What colour is Little Grey Rabbit's teapot?

2. What dreadful news does Hedgehog deliver with the milk?

3. What does Little Grey Rabbit wave at Wise Owl for a truce?

4. How many ducks does Little Grey Rabbit
see waddling across the road?

5. What does Little Grey Rabbit take with her
to rescue Squirrel and Hare from the weasel?

How Little Grey Rabbit Got Back Her Tail

1. Who pops out of the ground when
Little Grey Rabbit is picking primroses?
2. What does Hare wrap round his head when he's unwell?
3. What does Wise Owl ask for,
in exchange for Little Grey Rabbit's tail?
4. What book does Wise Owl give to Little Grey Rabbit?
5. Who saves the day and makes sure
Little Grey Rabbit gets back her tail?

The Great Adventure of Hare

1. What does Hare ask Little Grey Rabbit to fetch for his adventure?
2. What does Wise Owl take from Hare as payment for directions?
3. Who lives in Bilberry Wood?
4. What time does Hare tell the animals
in the teasel field to meet him?
5. When Hare arrives back in the
teasel field, who does he find there?

177

THE STORY OF FUZZYPEG THE HEDGEHOG

1. Which season is Fuzzypeg's birthday in?
2. What present does Hedgehog give to Fuzzypeg?
3. What creature does Hedgehog rescue Speckledy Hen from?
4. What game does Fuzzypeg play with Hare?
5. Who digs Fuzzypeg out from under the plant pot?

SQUIRREL GOES SKATING

1. What does Little Grey Rabbit find
   to rub on Hare's chilblains?
2. What does Little Grey Rabbit pack
   in the basket for their skating trip?
3. Where do Little Grey Rabbit, Squirrel
   and Hare hide the key to their house?
4. Can you spot the hungry rooks at lunchtime? How many are there?
5. How does Squirrel teach Rat a lesson?

LITTLE GREY RABBIT'S CHRISTMAS

1. What does Hare like catching on his tongue?

2. Who is inside the talking snowball?

3. What does Little Grey Rabbit fill the stockings with?

4. What surprise does Moldy Warp have for the woodland animals?

5. What presents are found in the sledge?

Answers

The Squirrel, the Hare and the Little Grey Rabbit

1. *Brown (p.24)* **2**. *A weasel is living in the wood (p.25)*
3. *A white handkerchief (p.32)* **4**. *Five (p.37)* **5**. *Pair of scissors, a rope and stick (p.38)*

How Little Grey Rabbit Got Back Her Tail

1. *Moldy Warp (p.51)* **2**. *A red handkerchief (p.53)* **3**. *A bell (p.62)*
4. *A (green) book of riddles (p.62/63)* **5**. *Moldy Warp (p.69)*

The Great Adventure of Hare

1. *His walking stick (p.74)* **2**. *Coat buttons (p.80)* **3**. *A fox (p.81)*
4. *Half-past twelve (p.82)* **5**. *Four sleepy rabbits and a hedgehog (p.94)*

The Story of Fuzzypeg the Hedgehog

1. *Summer (p.100)* **2**. *Glow-worms (p.107)* **3**. *An adder (p.108)*
4. *Noughts and crosses (p.111)* **5**. *Moldy Warp (p.120/121)*

Squirrel Goes Skating

1. *Frost from the grass (p.128)* **2**. *Sandwiches, plus an extra loaf
for the hungry rooks (p.132)* **3**. *On the window sill (p.135)*
4. *Top right/two (p.139)* **5**. *By tying a knot in his tail (p.144/145)*

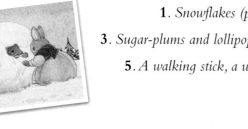

Little Grey Rabbit's Christmas

1. *Snowflakes (p.152/153)* **2**. *Fuzzypeg (p.158)*
3. *Sugar-plums and lollipops (p.165)* **4**. *A Christmas tree (p.169/170)*
5. *A walking stick, a wooden spoon, box with a thimble (p.171)*